Based on the Story by E. T. A. Hoffmann

THE Nutcracker

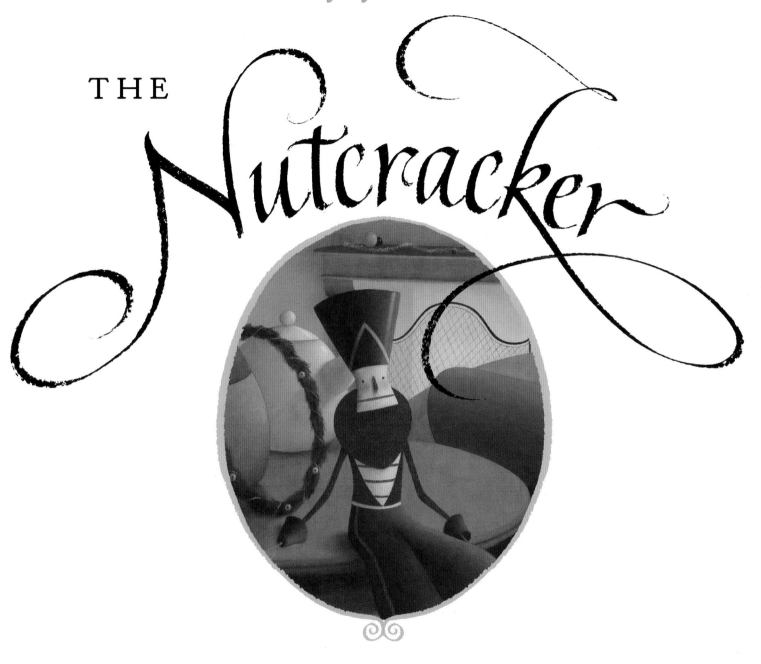

Retold by JOHN CECH   Illustrated by ERIC PUYBARET

STERLING

New York / London

ON CHRISTMAS EVE, Marie and her brother, Fritz, celebrated the holiday, as they did every year, with their parents and their godfather, Drosselmeier. The children waited on pins and needles while elaborate preparations went on behind the closed doors of the drawing room. In the space between the doors and the floor, the children could see shimmering lights and quick shadows. They could hear the rustling of paper and the swish of the fir tree's limbs as someone brushed against them, and they could smell gingerbread and pine, oranges and cinnamon filling the house. Then at last Mama and Papa, full of smiles, pulled open the doors with great fanfare. They invited Marie and Fritz to enter the room and see what they and Godfather Drosselmeier had been doing all that time.

In the center of the room sat a splendid tree, decorated with sugared almonds and a rainbow of candies, ornaments, garlands, and golden and silver apples. Candles lit every branch, sparkling like little stars in the sky. So many presents lay beneath the tree that the children could hardly take them all in—dolls and toy soldiers, a stuffed fox, a clown, a china pony, picture books—why, there were just too many things to name them all.

On a table to the side, nestled under a golden cloth, was Godfather Drosselmeier's present. Beaming, he lifted the curtain to reveal a magnificent toy palace, perfect right down to each shining glass window and each tile on its rooftop. Every year Drosselmeier created something special for the children, but this year's present was better than any that had come before. The palace had golden towers, and candlelight shimmered in its many windows, which, along with the doors, were open so that the children could look in from every direction. Inside, a grand ball was taking place, and everyone was dancing, twirling around and around. Among the many little figures, none taller than a thumb, were those that looked like Marie and Fritz, Mama and Papa, and even a tiny man in a long, green coat—a miniature Godfather Drosselmeier. When the dancing and music slowed, Godfather Drosselmeier wound the key on the base of the palace and the waltzes began again. After some time, the children grew tired and bleary-eyed, and drifted away to be surprised by their other presents. Marie's mother didn't want Drosselmeier's feelings to be hurt when the children left, and so she asked him to explain how he made this ingenious device, which he happily did, and in great detail.

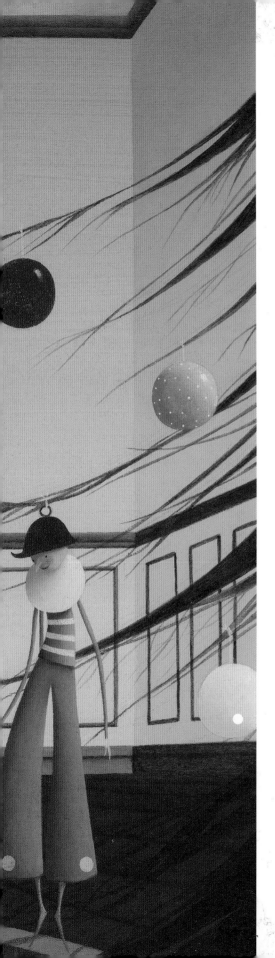

Among the toys and games and books, Marie noticed a strange figure. He was made from wood and stood straight and tall. A splendid uniform was painted on his body, and he had very large eyes, teeth, and lower jaw. Marie had never seen anything like him before, and for some reason she didn't understand she began to carry him around like one of her dolls.

"What is he?" she asked Godfather Drosselmeier.

"Oh, he's here to perform a very important duty this evening. Let me show you." Drosselmeier took the little man from Marie, opened his wooden jaw wide, placed a walnut in it, and pulled a lever on the little man's back. The nut cracked, and its pieces fell into Drosselmeier's outstretched palm.

"Let me try it!" Fritz shouted, rushing over from the other side of the room. And in moments, Fritz was busily cracking every nut in the dish. When he hit a Brazil nut that wouldn't yield, he pushed even harder on the lever, and with a snap, broke the teeth of the unfortunate nutcracker.

Marie pushed Fritz away as tears filled her eyes, and she cradled the wounded nutcracker in her arms.

"You didn't have to break him!" she cried.

"It's not my fault," Fritz shot back. "He's just not very strong."

Eventually the party wound down, just like Drosselmeier's toy. It was time for bed. Godfather Drosselmeier left, with a flourish of his green cape. Fritz scurried off to his room carrying a toy trumpet. Marie's mother and father yawned as they took away the dishes, and then blew out the candles on the tree and in the window.

"Come, Marie," her mother whispered, and held out her hand. "It's time for sleep."

"I'd like to stay up just a little longer," Marie insisted. "Please..."

She was looking into the large glass cupboard that held the children's many toys on the lower shelves. The intricate presents that Drosselmeier had given the family were on the upper shelves, just out of the children's reach so that they would not get broken. Marie had wrapped a ribbon around the head and chin of the injured nutcracker and placed it among Fritz's cavalry, using the bed of her doll, Clara, as its cot.

"All right," her mother said. "Since it's a special occasion. But just a few minutes longer."

The house grew quiet around Marie as she watched over the injured nutcracker resting inside the cupboard. She had not been there long when shadows began to climb the walls around her, and she turned to see a hundred spots of light moving toward her.

Mice. Everywhere.

The mice crawled from behind the walls and squeezed under the doors. From holes and cracks, they crept into the room. The hearthstone by the fireplace slowly lifted, and from beneath it appeared the biggest mouse of all. He had seven hideous heads with a crown on each one.

"I am the Mouse King!" the creature proclaimed. "We have come to eat your candy. We'll gobble up your cakes, and dine on your pies, and munch on every cashew in the house. And if you stand in our way, we'll nibble on your toes!"

Marie didn't know where to turn. She threw a pillow at the mice, but they scattered and regrouped. She picked up a footstool to keep them at bay, like she'd seen the lion tamer do at the circus, but still the mice poured into the room and surrounded Marie.

"Stand aside!" the Mouse King cried. The air whistled between his yellow teeth as he moved closer to Marie.

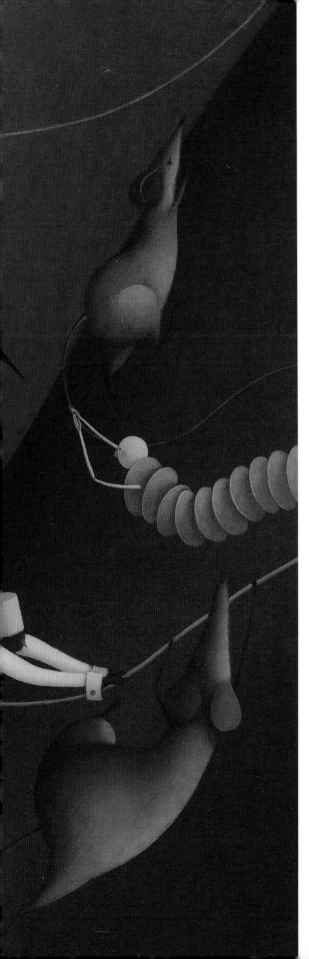

Marie backed up into the cabinet. Inside, she heard a rustling, like someone knocking on the glass, but she couldn't turn to see what it was without taking her eyes off the Mouse King, who was ready to pounce. From behind, she felt the door open and something ran out—a soldier. And then another, and another. Soon a whole army had massed itself in front of Marie to face the mice—soldiers of every kind, along with stuffed animals and dolls, clowns, jumping jacks, and acrobats. And in the very front of the toy army stood the Nutcracker, his silver sword poised to lead the charge.

Marie could not say exactly what happened next, but the battle was ferocious: fur flew and clowns' hats sailed into the sky, but at the end of it all, out of the smoke and dust and the shouts of the toys and the squeaks of the mice, Marie saw the Nutcracker drive the mice out of the room. He followed them, and came back with the seven golden crowns of the Mouse King held high on his sword. Dropping to one knee, he presented the crowns to Marie.

"Please accept these," the Nutcracker said, offering her the crowns, "as a token of my feelings for you. You cared for me when I was broken and no one else paid any attention to me. I would have remained in pieces if not for your kind heart."

"I'm glad that you're feeling better," Marie said, blushing just a little. "Fritz didn't mean any harm, really."

"I've spent this evening in your house. Would you now like to visit my land?" the Nutcracker asked.

"Oh, yes," Marie replied. As she said this, the walls of her house dissolved. Waiting outside was a sled. The Nutcracker easily helped Marie step into it, for he had grown much taller during the battle. Up they flew through clouds and snowflakes, across the deep blue night sky with its millions of glimmering stars. They might have flown for hours or seconds, years or days. Marie could not tell. She was lost in the breathless speed of their journey. And then they landed, and the sled carried them through a lovely countryside, along lanes lined with snow-white trees and over low, rolling hills, right up to the main doorway of a palace that looked exactly like the one that Godfather Drosselmeier had brought earlier in the evening, which now seemed so long ago.

"This is my home," the Nutcracker said. "And everyone is waiting for us."

He helped Marie out of the carriage and into the palace, where they were surrounded by the happy inhabitants of the Nutcracker's land. They escorted Marie and the Nutcracker to the two golden chairs of honor in the ballroom and then performed for them the most amazing dances. Sugarplum fairies let themselves down on gossamer threads from the sky itself. Harlequins somersaulted one over the other, leaping higher and higher. Young women in costumes that made them seem to be swans floated above the marble floor of the palace, never touching it. Turkish dancers spun so fast they moved like tops across the floor. Chinese acrobats balanced on their fingertips on the red noses of friendly dragons. It was all so exciting and wonderful, so giddy and breath-taking—like nothing Marie had ever seen before.

And she knew, somehow, in some deep way, that this was where she belonged.

Marie awoke in her bed on Christmas morning with a throbbing headache and a sore throat.

"What a night you've had," her mother said, and gently placed a cold compress on Marie's hot forehead. "We found you asleep on the floor, with all the toys around you. Mice must have gotten into the house, because they have been at the cookies and candy. They left such a mess. Thank goodness they're gone!"

"The Nutcracker chased them away with the other toys," Marie managed to say in a scratchy voice.

"Oh, Marie. Thank goodness your imagination doesn't have a cold!" her mother said in her kindest I-know-you're-making-this-up voice.

"But it's true," Marie exclaimed. "They *did* chase the mice away! And the Nutcracker was their leader. He defeated that nasty mouse with the seven heads, and then he took me to visit his land."

"That poor nutcracker," Marie's mother said, "isn't ready to lead anything, not with his jaw bandaged and his teeth about to fall out."

"But look at the seven crowns of the Mouse King that the Nutcracker gave me!" Marie cried, showing her mother the tiny golden crowns.

"Now, dear. Are you sure it wasn't Godfather Drosselmeier who gave these crowns to you a long time ago? He gives you and Fritz so many presents, we can't keep track of them all. Really, he's spoiled you two since you were babies."

Marie was quiet. What was the use of insisting when she knew her mother wouldn't believe her?

Later that morning, the door creaked open and Godfather Drosselmeier tiptoed into the room. He was carrying the bag that held his tools.

"How's our patient?" he asked. "I've come to wish you a happy Christmas and to fix your nutcracker. Your mama tells me he was in a battle last night." Drosselmeier winked at her, as if to say he understood and was on her side.

"Then you do believe me?" Marie asked him.

"Of course, my dear," Drosselmeier replied. "I've seen many things, and an army of toys fighting off an army of mice doesn't surprise me at all. You've had a very rare experience. You saw the toys come to life. Few people ever do. Now, let's see about fixing your nutcracker, and I'll tell you his story."

LONG, LONG AGO, a king and queen lived in a palace. Theirs was a very large palace, and they had a little daughter, whom they named Princess Pirlipat. She was the prettiest baby anyone had ever seen, and they all cooed over her constantly.

One day their palace was overrun by mice. The creatures were everywhere. The king and queen were so afraid that Pirlipat might get bitten by the mice that they posted guards of cats in the nursery to protect her. But the cats were no match for the mice, especially the queen of the mice, who consumed everything in the kitchen and the pantry and even ate up the curtains. Night after night the mice kept at it, steadily working their way toward the nursery where Princess Pirlipat slept.

The king didn't know what to do, so he asked my great, great, great uncle Drosselmeier, who was the court wizard and clock maker, for advice.

"Ah, Your Majesty," Drosselmeier replied. "I'm glad you asked. I have a young nephew who is fearless and clever and may be just the man to deal with this rodent."

That night, young Drosselmeier, who looked very much like your nutcracker here—did I tell you that?—waited, sword in hand, to defend the young princess. At precisely the stroke of midnight, the Mouse Queen reared her ugly head from beneath the flagstones of the hearth in the nursery.

"We'll make micemeat out of you," she hissed at young Drosselmeier. But he stood his ground and drew his sword and bravely drove the Mouse Queen away from Princess Pirlipat. The Mouse Queen was almost at the door when suddenly she stopped to face young Drosselmeier. She drew herself up to her full height and spat out these words:

> *Princess Pirlipat won't be a beauty,*
> *She'll be an ugly little bore.*
> *Only he who cracks the hardest nut,*
> *Can change her back as she was before.*

Then, leaving this curse behind her, the Mouse Queen vanished through the door and was never seen again. Some say the cats got her, but all they ever found was her empty crown in the hallway of the palace.

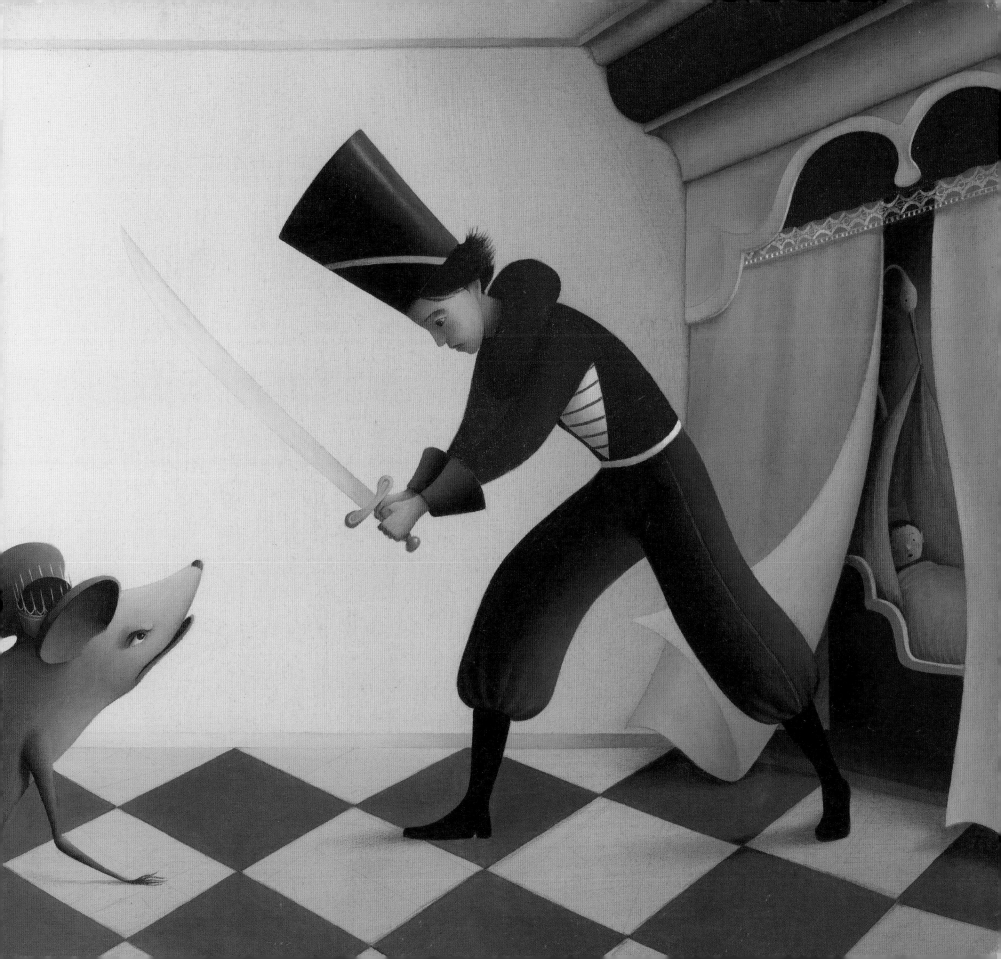

When the king and queen went to comfort Princess Pirlipat, who was crying loudly in her cradle, they discovered that she had indeed been transformed from a beautiful little girl into a very unattractive child. It's hard to imagine an ugly baby, but Princess Pirlipat had become truly unsightly.

What did this mean? The king and queen consulted the wisest people in the kingdom, but none knew how to untangle the spell of the Mouse Queen.

"Since you brought this curse upon us," said the king to young Drosselmeier, "it is you who must lift it, or be forever banished from this kingdom."

Drosselmeier returned to his uncle in despair. "What can I do," he cried. "Where do I begin?"

His uncle, who was a very wise man, thought and thought and thought. He consulted every book in his library, and in everybody else's libraries, too. Finally, he brought young Drosselmeier his advice. "You must first find the hardest nut there is, and then find a way to crack it. After that, the rest should be easy."

So young Drosselmeier set out to discover the hardest nut to crack. He journeyed far and wide for many years but could not find a nut that he could not crack with his own teeth. It's true, he had very strong teeth, but even so, all the nuts he found were easy. Walnuts and pecans, peanuts and pistachios, macadamias and almonds, hazelnuts and hickories, pili nuts and pandanuses. Some of the nuts were so bitter that even the birds wouldn't eat them, and some of them were sweet as candy. In Brazil he found guaranas that kept him up all night, and in Australia he found quandongs that even a hammer couldn't open, they said. But they all cracked quickly between his jaws. One day, as young Drosselmeier was visiting China, he realized that he would never find the hardest nut by wandering around the world. He might as well go home and face his fate.

Young Drosselmeier returned to his uncle's home late one evening, weary from the road and resigned to his destiny. "The king will send me away," he said tearfully to his uncle, "and we'll probably never see each other again."

"Don't despair," his uncle replied. "A curious thing has happened, but I didn't know how to find you to tell you. One day while you were away, a peddler came to my door selling nuts for the holidays. I bought a sack from him and cracked every one of them except for this one. Nothing could make a dent in it—not a mallet or a stone or even a horse's iron hooves. I know because I tried them all. Just look at this—the nut even has a name cut into its shell." He held up a glass so that his nephew could read the word: "Crack-a-Took."

"This must be the nut I have been searching for," young Drosselmeier exclaimed. "We should go to the castle immediately!"

"No," said his uncle, who was a very clever man. "Let's wait. If I bring this nut to the king, he's sure to hold a competition to see who can crack it. Just stay out of sight for a little while longer, until we see what the king is offering as a reward. Do you think that you can crack this?"

"Uncle, I've been cracking nuts for years—some of them as hard as stones—and I've never had to bite twice. This nut will be no different."

The next day young Drosselmeier's uncle took Crack-a-Took to the king and told him how he had found and tested it. The king was delighted and sent his heralds out to announce a royal contest to crack the nut. Whoever did so would claim his daughter's hand in marriage and with it a large sack of treasure.

In the time that young Drosselmeier had been away, Princess Pirlipat had grown up into a young woman, but she had not lost any of the unattractive features with which the Mouse Queen had cursed her. This made the princess mean. Mad and mean.

And yet young men came from afar to win her and the reward. But the young men left just as quickly as they arrived, with aching teeth and swollen jaws. No one could match his molars against Crack-a-Took. Some even had to be carried out of the throne room in a swoon after trying to open the nut. Finally, in desperation, the king offered the princess and his kingdom to the man who could split Crack-a-Took.

"Now is the time," Drosselmeier's uncle told his nephew. They returned to the palace the next day, and young Drosselmeier was presented to the king, the queen, and Princess Pirlipat. "I am not an unreasonable man," the king replied. "And from the look of him, it certainly seems as though your nephew has been searching long and hard. He may have his chance."

The king motioned the men-at-arms to approach more closely and have the stretcher ready, just in case. Princess Pirlipat barely noticed young Drosselmeier—she was glancing at a book and yawning.

"Now, Nephew," Drosselmeier's uncle warned, "if you're lucky enough to split Crack-a-Took, there's one last part to lifting the curse. I have this on the best authority. You must give the kernel of the nut to the princess on one knee, and then close your eyes, stand up, and take seven steps backward without opening them. Only then will the spell be broken. But you must do everything right, or the curse will fall from the princess onto you!"

Young Drosselmeier picked up the nut from its place on a purple pillow that sat on top of a column in the middle of the throne room. He placed it between his teeth and bit down slowly, pressing his jaws together. There was a terrible cracking sound in the room, like a large tree snapping in a storm. "My goodness!" cried the queen. "He's broken his jaw!"

Young Drosselmeier cupped his hands under his chin, and let the shattered shell of Crack-a-Took fall into it, the round, glowing kernel still intact and ready for the princess. Carefully removing the kernel, he placed it on the royal pillow, approached the princess, kneeled, and offered it to her with a smile. Now the princess was paying attention, as she plucked the kernel of the nut and popped it into her mouth. Instantly, her ugliness melted away and she became beautiful once more.

"Remember, nephew, what you still have to do," Drosselmeier's uncle reminded him.

Closing his eyes and standing up, young Drosselmeier kept his balance and took six steps backward. But on the seventh step, he tripped on the toe of someone who had been jumping excitedly in the air and waving his hands without realizing that he was in young Drosselmeier's way.

Just as suddenly as Princess Pirlipat had become beautiful, the unfortunate young Drosselmeier's head grew quite large, his teeth very big, and his eyes enormous.

This new young Drosselmeier was not at all the kind of man that the king wanted his daughter to marry, much less the kind of man who should become the next king. And so the king put off announcing his daughter's engagement, and put off announcing his successor, and put off rewarding young Drosselmeier. He simply shook his hand and left him standing in the throne room, alone and speechless.

"What injustice!" young Drosselmeier said when he was back at his uncle's house. "How can he break his promise like that?"

"Well, kings will do what kings will do," Drosselmeier's uncle said philosophically, and added, "Don't say anything rash, and don't do anything foolish. Just bide your time."

And so young Drosselmeier did bide his time, keeping watch year after year for seven-headed mice, waiting for the day that someone would lift the curse that was placed on him after he cracked Crack-a-Took and stumbled on his seventh step. And although the king did not honor him, the people of the kingdom did, and made nutcrackers out of wood to look just like young Drosselmeier did when he defeated the Mouse Queen.

And that, dear Marie, is where all nutcrackers began," Godfather Drosselmeier said. "I have this on the best authority from my uncle, who heard it from his uncle, who heard it from his uncle—who was the court's wizard. And here is your nutcracker again, and he is quite sound, as you can see, ready to finish off the next plate of nuts there is to crack."

"But if the nutcracker can crack any nut, how did Fritz break the Nutcracker's teeth?" Marie asked Godfather Drosselmeier.

"Well, it's a great mystery, but sometimes little brothers can manage to break anything," he replied.

"But how can I remove the curse? I know I must help him!" Marie cried. And now tears filled her eyes.

"Well, the only way to do that," Drosselmeier said, trying to comfort her, "is to bide your time and to never lose faith in those dreams you once had— the ones you know were real, no matter what anyone else says! Just bide your time, and you'll see."

Godfather Drosselmeier was right about the nutcracker. He never broke again, and he stood watch over Marie and her house, her dolls and toys and books, and even Fritz's toy soldiers. He always kept his eyes wide open, ready for anything.

Marie grew up, but she never forgot that journey she made to visit the Nutcracker's land. Each Christmas, the nutcracker left the cabinet to take up his special place at the family's parties, and each year Marie looked at him and wondered about that evening long ago.

When Marie was eighteen, Godfather Drosselmeier, whose hair by then had turned snow-white, gave the family a fantastic sleigh ride toy. When it was wound, the sleigh drifted through toy clouds to a magical country, and then through the hills and valleys of the toy countryside to a palace where a party was in progress. Drosselmeier looked at Marie when he set the enchanted mechanism into motion, and smiled warmly and mysteriously.

That night, after everyone had left, Marie stayed up looking at the nutcracker. "I love you, nutcracker," she said, "and I always have." Then she set the nutcracker on the table with her other presents, and fell asleep in the chair in front of the fire.

When Marie awoke it was Christmas morning. Everything was just as she had left it, except that the nutcracker was gone. Marie looked everywhere, but no one had seen it, not even Fritz, who was practicing his trumpet concerto to play for everyone later that day.

"It could be those mice again," Marie's mother said, jokingly. "They've come back after ten years!"

The morning slowly passed into afternoon. Suddenly there was a commotion at the front door as Godfather Drosselmeier appeared for Christmas dinner. With him was a guest, a young man who looked a little like Godfather Drosselmeier might have looked when he was young. But he also looked quite a bit like the nutcracker—the same cloak and boots, the same hat—only his were not made of wood. And there was nothing wooden or exaggerated about the young man's face. Indeed it was quite handsome.

"Let me present to you, dear people, my nephew, who's come to join me here. Despite his young years, he's had many adventures, and I hope you'll make him welcome."

Young Drosselmeier looked at Marie, kissed her hand, and said, "Thank you, Marie."

At that, Marie knew that he was indeed her Nutcracker and the curse had been broken at last. "You're welcome, Mr. Drosselmeier," she said, blushing. "Oh, you're most welcome."

STERLING and the distinctive Sterling logo are registered trademarks of
Sterling Publishing Co., Inc.

LIBRARY OF CONGRESS CATALOGING-IN-PUBLICATION DATA

Cech, John.
The nutcracker / based on the story by E.T.A. Hoffmann ; retold by John Cech ;
illustrated by Eric Puybaret.
p. cm.
Summary: In this retelling of the original 1816 German story, Godfather Drosselmeier gives young Marie
a nutcracker for Christmas, and she finds herself in a magical realm where she saves a boy from an evil curse.
ISBN 978-1-4027-5562-0
[1. Fairy tales. 2. Christmas-Fiction.] I. Puybaret, Eric, ill. II. Hoffmann, E. T. A. (Ernst Theodor Amadeus),
1776-1822. Nussknacker und Mauskönig. III. Title.
PZ8.C293Nu 2009
[E]-dc22

2008043084

2 4 6 8 10 9 7 5 3 1

Published by Sterling Publishing Co., Inc., 387 Park Avenue South, New York, NY 10016
Text © 2009 by John Cech
Illustrations © 2009 by Eric Puybaret
Distributed in Canada by Sterling Publishing
c/o Canadian Manda Group,
165 Dufferin Street, Toronto, Ontario, Canada M6K 3H6
Distributed in the United Kingdom by GMC Distribution Services
Castle Place, 166 High Street, Lewes, East Sussex, England BN7 1XU
Distributed in Australia by Capricorn Link (Australia) Pty. Ltd.
P.O. Box 704, Windsor, NSW 2756, Australia

Printed in China

The illustrations in this book were done using acrylic on linen.
The display lettering and decorative devices were created by Judythe Sieck.
The text type was set in McKenna Handletter.
Designed by Judythe Sieck

Sterling ISBN 978-1-4027-5562-0

For information about custom editions, special sales, premium and corporate purchases,
please contact Sterling Special Sales Department at 800-805-5489 or
specialsales@sterlingpublishing.com.